FREAKYBUTTRUE'S

STELLA'S
BABY-SITTING
SERVICE

STELLA'S BABY-SITTING SERVICE

BY MIKE WELLINS

ILLUSTRATED BY
COLIN BATTY

A FREAKYBUTTRUE PUBLICATION
PORTLAND, OREGON

Resounding thanks to Lisa Freeman for all her hard work and invaluable input. Thanks also to Christa Lewis and Jim Hardison for their proofing and editing. Double huge thanks to Colin Batty for his amazing art that inspired and brought this story to life.

*"Fear is a slinking cat I find beneath
the lilacs of my mind."*

- Sophie Tunnell

ISBN 9781453745502

All rights reserved. Published by
Freakybuttrue
Portland, Oregon.

Printed in the USA

stellasbabysittingservice.com

CONTENTS

PROLOGUE 9

THE STRANGE CASE OF MRS.
CAMERON'S MEATLOAF 23

HOT CLUES ON A COLD
SLIMY TRAIL 37

THE CLUES TAKE US TO
THE NECROPOLIS 42

FURTHER AND FURTHER FROM
HOME WE GET 49

INTO THE BELLY OF THE BEAST:
THE FOOD COURT 57

WE ARE NOT ALONE 69

SEARCH AND DESTROY 79

THROUGH THE EYE OF THE
NEEDLE 83

EPILOGUE 100

PROLOGUE

I f you are reading this, then I must be dead, dead tired that is, of all the annoyances I must deal with on a daily basis. This is investigating reporter, Stella Louise Sedgewick, reporting from my bedroom in the majorly decrepit and twisted town of Trickle Falls. It's a very modern town, with everything in neat rows, and nothing on the surface that looks old and is instead covered with shiny bright plastic. There are whole neighborhoods where people all mow their yards in the same direction and frown at their neighbors when someone plants the wrong flowers or paints their front door too dark of color.

Trickle Falls is a town devoid of character, with a bunch of people who seem incapable of entertaining themselves for very long. The greatest fake detective of all time, Sherlock Holmes once said something to this effect: "When you have eliminated the impossible, whatever remains, however improbable, must be the truth." And that is what I have concluded after studying this town and the surrounding area. It is true. A whole town can truly be unable to entertain itself if something is not going on that causes everyone to run around like maniacs for.

When you drive into most cities or towns, there's a big wooden sign that says, "Welcome to our town," whatever it may be, and then below the name of the town usually is one phrase that says something interesting about the town or what it's famous for. "Welcome to Somewhere-ville, home of the world's loudest peanut brittle oven." Or "You're entering north Any Town, first in unicycling." But for Trickle Falls, there isn't anything there; no sentence that Trickle Falls is known for, probably because the guys building the sign had to leave early to go to a pumpkin carving contest or the corn maze at the Fall Carnival. Maybe the people designing the sign didn't even think of adding a line describing our little town because they were all sleepy and full after a pie eating contest.

If there was a little sentence on our city sign, I think it would say, "Welcome to Trickle Falls. We're bored." That would be about right. This reporter is suspicious of people who say, "I'm bored." How is that possible? Bored on a planet in this universe, with all the stuff around us, below us, flying through the air, swimming through the water? And that's just the stuff we know about. Beyond the known is the unknown, and that's where I want to be, poking it with a stick.

Regardless of my desires to search the dark reaches of this planet and beyond, for the time being, I'm stuck in Trickle Falls for reasons so lame that it makes my eye throb to think about it, and this time of year makes my eye throb even more. Oh, I can't wait until I get my driver's license.

Every year, like clockwork, this time comes when there aren't any holidays in the immediate area for everyone to run around like idiots for. It's more than a month before our next parade for everyone to go all stupid over, and there's no looming carnival for everyone to get all excited about. So, for the time being and the near future, there's no cake-walking, no churro-eating, no cone-dipping, no cotton-candying, no dunk-tanking and no corn-dogging. To be specific, to the horror of everyone in this town, there are also no Regionals, there are no Nationals, there are no play-offs, there are no bowls, there are no semi-finals or finals. There's no Ferris-wheeling, no ring-tossing, no jam-judging, no tug-of-warring, and no roller-coastering, much to this reporter's relief.

Trickle Falls is a thousand foot long baby, and as long as someone is dangling a colorful Thanksgiving parade or a pancake feed in front of its face, it's happy, but as soon as the mobile comes down, that baby starts to squirm, fidget, cry and eventually starts to do real damage. I don't like babies, especially a thousand foot one. There's nothing to dangle in front of that baby right now. This lull in color, noise, crazy foods and activities has left the witless minions of Trickle Falls desperate; and this will cause them to act irrationally.

If we are to learn anything from history, we know that this time of calm has the opposite effect on the shopping drones of Trickle Falls. It was exactly this time of year, three years ago, when the great cat shave incident rocked the neighborhood. Case number 10-34C:

Victim number one: Bonkers, the Miller's kitty,

Victim #1 "BONKERS"

completely shaved in the dead of night. No fur was ever found and I am told that an emergency sweater had to be knitted for Bonkers because of the early winter that year. Then, the following night, victim number two, the Peterson's cat Jerry, who enjoys string, napping and shredding rolls of toilet paper, was found unharmed but with all his hair neatly and completely removed. People were upset and even more so when, over the next two nights, the Emerson's cat, Mr. Smellybottom, and finally victim number four, the Buchanan's cat, Dutch were also shaved.

Victim #2 "JERRY"

Victim #3 "MR. SMELLYBOTTOM"

Victim #4 "DUTCH"

Four innocent cats, shaved against their will, on four consecutive nights. Pet owners began to fear for their fur. Pft! It was an easy case for me.

With good surveillance, several solid tips and a certain trash can with tell-tale hair and some glue, the culprit was easily spotted by this reporter.

However, all alerting emails and phone calls sent to the Trickle Falls Police Department, the Mayor's office, Animal Control, and even the *Trickle Times Standard*, our local newspaper, went unanswered. Eventually the police put two and two together. So, it was no surprise to this reporter when the culprit, Mrs. Hildegard Arden-Schuller, on a bright sunny day, was quietly escorted to a white van outside her beautiful house on Juniper Court, wearing the hat she'd made of all the cat hair. I'm told she's taking a good long rest up state at Mindbruken Acres.

Why then, you may ask, did I not receive more credit for my discovery?

It's not unheard of for such deeds to earn a public commendation or perhaps the key to the city, or even a working lunch with the Mayor! Why are all my emails and letters completely ignored? Is it because I'm not old, or is it that people just don't want to know the truth because the truth is just too scary? A few times, I've gone down to the editor's office of the local paper, and even tried to see the Mayor and the Police Chief, in person, but that always makes it worse because my left eye sets everyone off. So what? I have a red eye. Get over it. This reporter is not bothered by such lame reactions; there is too much serious work to be done.

My personal idol and inspiration is, of course, the greatest hunter of truth in the history of supernatural exploration and study. He was a true and intrepid explorer of all things ignored by modern science. He is none other than the late, great Charles Fort.

Mr. Fort was the first true journalist to seek the truth, no matter what scary form it took. Google him, you'll see. I follow his solid tradition of exploration and investigation.

Who knows, perhaps someday I will put all my cases and stories into a book too, my own "Book of the Danged." And by danged, I mean topics and occurrences so scary and inexplicable that they are danged by modern society, science and the media, which means they are simply ignored.

It's fear; it's the fear of the unknown that makes people look away from what they can't explain, but not for me. I'll be, like Mr. Charles Fort, danged before I give up. Charles Fort was there when it rained frogs and warm rocks out of a clear blue sky, he was there when hailstones fell that were as big as elephants and he was there when sailors chased a giant sea monster in the South Pacific. I'll carry that torch and be there when the unexplained happens, taking notes and

taking photos whenever possible.

Still, you have to be careful when you begin to dig in Trickle Falls. It's like the time I watched old man Pappas sitting at a bus stop digging under one of his thick, brown toenails. First, it's all just normal skin cells and blue sock lint, but then the deeper he goes, you soon see that there's other stuff in there, black stuff, some of it obviously dried blood cells and dirt, but what is the rest of that stuff? Where does it come from? And it seems like you can just keep digging deeper and deeper beside that toenail and it never ends, and there's always more and more black stuff.

That's how it is around here. And nowhere else is this phenomenon more obvious than in this reporter's own house, where I live, crammed in behind my own personal giant toenail with my so-called "family". Ugh. Actually, my parents are fine. It's my siblings I have issue with.

More importantly, there are other, far more sinister forces at work in this smear of a town. Rumors of ghostly lights out by the washout, and strange apparitions in and around the giant cheese at the playground have the pre-schoolers in a real panic. It was the intent of this reporter to explore this incident and stake out the playground with round-the-clock surveillance. Instead, reality calls, and I'm forced to work my day job as a juvenile restraint and containment specialist, or as my clients call it, a babysitter. Ugh! That word makes me want to spit! I don't sit babies. I won't client any punk who can't go to the bathroom by himself, or walk or feed his fat little face without barfing. I hate babies, and I hate barf and barfing. Sooooo Gross. No, please Mrs. Smith, don't let little Jimmy have three root beer floats before I show up because I don't do barf.

Even though there's a sci-fi movie marathon on cable, I will tuck it in and go earn a few dollars at the cable-less Cavendish's house, just next door. Regrettably, they have one child, whom I'll refer to as Potato, the name this reporter gave him, and the only name I'll ever use. Why, you ask, why Potato? When you see him, you'll know why.

THE STRANGE CASE
OF MRS. CAMERON'S MEATLOAF

7:34 p.m.: I arrived early at the Cavendish's house. It took all my patience and calm to ring the doorbell. It is regrettable and unthinkable that I, an ace reporter, am reduced to such a low level of work, especially since breaking so many famous cases as I have. Sadly, my greatest investigating accomplishments, although spectacular and important, pay very little or nothing, but obviously I'm not in it for the money. Was Charles Fort rich? No, I don't think so, but he did invent a version of a checkers game on a board with thousands of squares. Pretty cool! I made a set, but no one will play with me.

7:41 p.m.: I was in position and began the evening's job. On the only positive note, I like Mrs. Cavendish, and she always tips me well for my work. She's not stupid; she's not going to mess with a good thing. What price is peace of mind? And how she could have produced a kid such as Potato is another mystery that would probably be too annoying to investigate.

Mrs. Cavendish let me in, and I moved into the kitchen where Potato sat, eating fish sticks. Mrs. Cavendish gave me all the standard numbers for her cell, the police, the fire department, all of which I had already committed to memory, years ago. Mrs. Cavendish was off in a cloud of perfume and make-up with one clear order: no dessert for Potato until he finishes his asparagus. I follow orders. It is the sacred bond between me and my client.

7:44 p.m.: Mrs. Cavendish was out the door and seconds later, Potato leaned back from the table, his face smeared with tartar sauce.

"Ooooowweeee, I am soooo full. Mom, what's for dessert?" The little blob slid from his chair, wiping his hands on his shirt. "Mom?" he squawked. The little troll had been so face in the food that he didn't even notice the changing of the guard. Now do you see what I mean about him being a Potato? It isn't that he's fat, which he is, in a sort of thick sort of way, but his head actually looks like a potato; he looks, acts and even thinks like a potato.

"Sorry Potato, but I have strict, detailed instructions from your mother; you aren't to have any dessert until you've finished the asparagus."

"Oh, it's you…" Potato pulled his face into a knot. He picked up his plate, smiling a big smile with food in his teeth. I was revolted. "I did, see? I did eat my asparagins."

I answered him firmly, "She didn't say anything about any plate. She said until you finish the asparagus." I slid over the dish on the table, teeming with the asparagus spears.

"What? No way!" Potato squealed with anger. "She meant what was on my plate, not what was in the whole bowl! That's what she meant; call her cell phone and check!"

I openly laughed in his wide flat face. "Are you kidding? I'm not bothering a client with something as stupid as that." I have never made a parent call while working in my entire career, and I was not going to now, especially about something as useless as that. Nope, not on my watch.

Potato was stubborn and crossed his thick arms and pulled a stupid pose. "You can't make me eat all that, no way, not now, not ever."

This reporter is used to hostile witnesses and suspects and played it cool. "You're right, I can't make you eat the asparagus, but I can stop you from eating dessert and playing *Shards of Death 6, Melee of Madness*."

Potato tried to hold firm, but his eyelid twitched. To make my point, I went to the refrigerator and took out the five-inch thick, lava fudge cake. I set it down and nibbled on a few crumbs.

Potato eyed the thick cake. "Oooowwww," he whined. "How about that meatloaf, can I eat that instead? I never had meatloaf! Is it good? It sounds good." He's so dense, it's not funny.

"Potato, what would be the point of me letting you eat something you like?"

Potato was confused. "But why do I have to eat stuff I don't like, then?"

I explained to him clearly and slowly. "Bad tasting food is how parents secretly punish their kids for ruining their weekends and evenings for the rest of their lives."

Potato gave up and laid his thick head on the table with a meaty thud. "Oh yeah, I forgot."

"And why on Earth does your mom have a whole extra dinner, anyway? I thought you had fish sticks."

Potato was too eager to fill in the details. "Oh yeah, it was a present from our new neighbors, The Gamaras. They just moved in. Isn't that great? Do you think they'll give us a meatloaf every day because I never had a meatloaf. I like spaghetti!"

I examined the foil-covered meatloaf on the counter. It looked fine. Attached was a note.

EXHIBIT "A"

Hello,
we're excited to move into the new neighborhood. I hope you enjoy this. It's just a little taste of things to come. I just know we'll be good friends.
Sincerely, Mrs. Cameron, your new neighbor

The Camerons? In all honesty, this reporter was a little annoyed that Potato had neighborhood information that I didn't. I wanted to see these new neighbors for myself, so I made a deal with Potato.

STRANGE ODOR

EXHIBIT "B"

"All right, you eat half of the asparagus and a piece of meatloaf, and then you can have dessert later. Now get started, double time!"

"Ohhhhhwwwwwww…" Potato whined as he climbed back up to his seat, pinched his nose and started to choke down the asparagus. I took the meatloaf, uncovered it and set it on the table.

7:56 p.m.: I went out to the front porch of the Cavendish's. The night was calm and quiet, visibility was good, and the wind was out of the Southeast at 2 or 3 kilometers per hour. Sure enough, their next-door neighbor to the North had the telltale signs of moving boxes in the driveway. I studied the house and saw all the normal signs of a new move-in. Briefly, I saw an older woman with gray hair puttering around inside.

It was curious. I knew more about Trickle Falls than anyone, and yet somehow I'd missed a move-in, just two houses down from mine? A certain informant of mine was going to feel the wrath of one of my famous, pointed emails.

From the kitchen I could hear the groans and whines of Potato as he choked his way through more asparagus.

Almost feeling sorry for the little bunion, I announced to him, "Okay Potato, I think you've had enough asparagus and I don't know if your mom is going to want you to cut into that meatloaf just yet."

7:58 p.m.: I stepped into the kitchen. This reporter cannot find words to convey the amount of shocktitude I felt when I saw what was in front of me. Mrs. Cameron's meatloaf had ballooned in size and was now the size of a mattress, covered with thick greasy gravy. It wiggled and oozed like a massive slug on the kitchen table as it attempted to choke down Potato, feet first. It would be a lie to say that terror didn't grip my brain, but the look on Potato's face was AWESOME!!! My training kicked into gear, and my first and instinctual thought was: CAMERA!!! I snapped a few pictures as the creature slowly sucked Potato in. My usual angle is to put my digital camera up in a safe place and then program it to take pictures, randomly. That's the great thing about digital cameras.

Potato was horrified and called out, "What kind of meatloaf is this?! Ahhhhhh, Stella, help me! Euuuuuwwww, it just oozed into my underpants! Stella, help!"

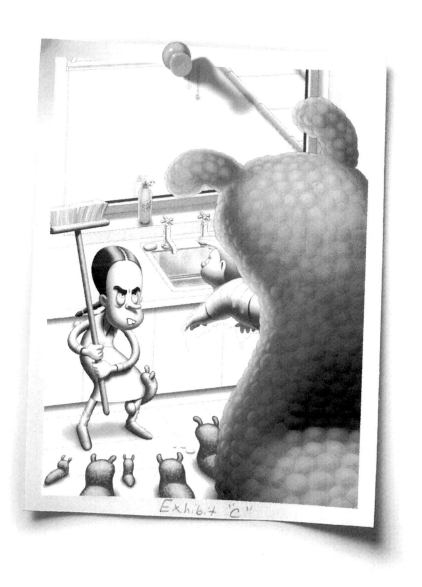

Exhibit "C"

I snapped a few more shots and then looked for a weapon to dispatch this entree of evil. In the nearby pantry, I discovered a sturdy broom and tried several, varied ninja-inspired attacks, but nothing worked. Potato, the wimp, was already getting weak and was starting to lose it as this main course of mayhem slowly absorbed him.

"Ooooohhhh, Stella, I'm getting sleepy, maybe I'll take a nap in this cozy sleeping bag." The thing moved slow and blob like, as plates and dishes went flying. The kitchen table creaked and moaned under the weight as more stuff crashed to the floor. Luckily, Mrs. Cavendish is used to Potato, the biggest klutz of all, so most of it was plastic. If I lived, there would be a real mess to clean up.

Charles Fort never gave up, and I was just as determined. No giant dish of destruction was going to get the better of me and devour my client. I tried new tactics, using a spray bottle, a bat, and a small ladder, but nothing worked. Every smart operative always knows when to call for back up, and I attempted just that and dialed 911.

As trained, I calmly and precisely reported the scene to the operator, all the while keeping the meatloaf, with stabs from a fireplace poker, from finishing off an unconscious Potato. On the phone, I was told that filing a false report including one with a "giant meatloaf" wasn't funny and was a crime, and I had ten seconds to get off the phone. I was off in two, exactly what I expected.

8:06 p.m. (approx.): The meatloaf had grown and was now the size of a baby hippopotamus, but uglier. I worried the kitchen table was going to collapse. To make matters worse, there were now little slug meat loaves forming on the surface of the big meatloaf. It was definitely trying to swallow Potato completely as it lumbered toward the sliding glass door, which was partly open. Potato was almost in up to his neck, and little meatloaves were sitting on his stupid eyelids. I wasn't seeing a really big tip that night from Mrs. Cavendish.

Something had to be done, so I moved quickly and cat-like, through the house and into the Cavendish's garage. I briefly considered an axe, a rake, a shovel and hoe, all with the same conclusion: then what? The creature is just too huge and gooey: what would an ax even do to it? Then I spotted the perfect instrument. Against the wall was the Mulch Master Yard King 9000 XR-9, a weed whip with the pulverizer attachment. I grabbed it and a pair of safety goggles and returned to the kitchen.

One pull and the Mulch Master roared to life. I jammed it into what I assumed was the brain, the part above Potato's head. The cutter tore through the slug skin like it was a water balloon. Goo poured out, covering Potato's face. The meatloaf, in pain, roared with anger and pulled away from the weed-eater. I took that moment to pull Potato out of the mouth area. He hit the floor and slid a few feet in the goo that was definitely not gravy. The Mulch Master did the trick, and the giant thing slid off the table and headed toward the open door. Stuff went flying everywhere.

Potato floundered in his own pool of goo before jumping up and running to the kitchen sink. He blasted his tongue under the running water. "Uck! I hate meatloaf!" From behind him, a smaller meatloaf attached to Potato's puffy leg. As expected, he completely freaked out and ran around the house, totally over-reacting. At that moment, this reporter had one slug on her calf and another on her upper arm but remained calm and collected despite the pain of the suction bite.

I was pulled away from the giant meatloaf to rescue Sprinkles, the Cavendish's cat, which was wearing a slug like a mini-skirt and howling like I've never heard. Several slugs were storming

the fish tank, eating the Lemon Tetra like snacks. Again, I fired up the Mulch Master and turned a bunch of gooey solids into runny liquids. Like a mongoose on energy drinks, we found the little meatloaf creatures all over the kitchen and family room and stopped their attack. The Mulch Master was a lethal weapon to them as they blorped and splattered on contact with the spinning pulverizer attachment. We squished at least twenty. I made a mental note that later I'd come and get samples for further analysis.

8:14 p.m.: After catching a quick breath and guzzling some water. I grabbed my camera. Technically it's my brother's, but a bet's a bet and I won fair and square. So what if he had to go to the emergency room? A bet is a bet.

I raced around, readying to give chase. I ordered Potato to his feet. "Let's go, mister! We've got to stay on that thing's trail!" I wanted to dash back to my house to get my detecting kit, but there was no time. Potato had wiped off most of the goo. I knew this was going to be a tough sell. Potato sat like a bump and wasn't budging.

"No way, Stella! That thing almost ate me, ate my cat, my fish, my dessert, what if I had lost my—" Finally a break: the little plug had stashed his Gamedude videogame in his back pocket! Potato frantically scrambled around the room, shrieking and whining as he hunted for his Gamedude, "My Gamedude! My Gamedude! It was in my back pocket! And that 'meat slug thing' It took my-- my Gamedude!"

HOT CLUES ON A COLD SLIMY TRAIL

I grabbed Potato by the scruff of his shirt and we headed out as I convinced him he had to come if we were to ever recover his Gamedude. Mega rule alpha: Never leave a client alone. Yes, I would have liked nothing more than ditch the little spud and go off on my own, but a deal is a deal, and this reporter gave her word.

Immediately outside, one would notice the darkness and lack of sun, as is typical of an early fall night. It wasn't cold. In fact it was eerily comfortable. It was as if the night was saying, "Come on out, it's very pleasant, but I have something unpleasant to show you." The warm wind blew and dried leaves seemed to be everywhere.

In the damp grass the thick trail of goo

went off the patio, through the sandbox and over the fence. We gave chase and I bounded over the fence into the Cameron's yard. With some huffing and puffing, a while later, Potato dropped over the fence too. The goo trail was hard to miss and moved across the yard, heading South-Southeast.

"There it goes!" Potato panted. I turned toward the thick trail of goo, but something twitched the hairs on my neck, and my eye throbbed. I caught a shape out of the corner of my eye. Slowly, I turned around. Something smelled strange, like nothing I've ever smelled before, a sickly smell.

Then I noticed, standing in the shadows beside the house was Mrs. Cameron, herself. She was a large woman with wild, wiry hair. She was dressed just like any grandma, but there was no way that she was just a grandma. She made no effort to hide and yet she didn't move, but instead stood looking at me with no expression, stroking her strange looking cat that she held in her arms. Potato was doing his best to get over the next fence and didn't see her.

In an instant, I had to choose. A rare problem for a reporter/investigator: too many leads! Do I confront Mrs. Cameron, or do I stay on the trail of that slug thing? My feet decided for me, but I did get off a shot from my camera, as evidence. I bounded over the fence, dragging Potato and tailing a meatloaf with a serious goo problem. I commanded Mrs. Cameron as I ran off.

"Mrs. Cameron, or whoever you are, I'm placing you under citizen's arrest for your part in the release of a yet to be identified creature. Please stay right where you are, and I will return for further questioning!" I just knew she wasn't going to follow my orders.

SUSPECT # 1 Mrs Cameron?

Behind her house, the trail was thick and easy to follow and flies were already finding the dried trail of slime. But somehow the meat slug picked up speed because the trail went on, always way ahead of us. We ran though lots and fields, gullies and culverts, alleys and parking lots. This was a hectic time for this reporter, and the action is a blur as we crossed town on foot, moving through the night.

We stopped in an alley and Potato panted for air. For the millionth time he said he was tired and his feet hurt. I had spotted a glowing light from around the corner, and I hoped Potato hadn't noticed, but across the street the glow of a neon restaurant sign was obvious.

"I smell French fries!" I tried to coax him to keep going, but he was insistent. "I've got four dollars of my own money and I'm getting something! If you want me to come with you, we're stopping and getting a snack! Gamedude or not, I just don't pass up French fries."

What could I do? An army marches on its stomach, although he had just eaten a full dinner and plenty of asparagus less than a half hour ago. We stopped for provisions for the moment, at Jasper's Burgershack for French fries and shave ice.

8:47 p.m.: We relaxed for a moment as I tasted the last drops of the delicious Blamo Double Cherry shave ice, I almost knew where this trail we were following would lead us, and a few hundred meters later, I was right. The trail took us through the parking lot, across a field, over the railroad tracks and into the moss covered gates of Pineboard Cemetery, the one place in Trickle Falls that wasn't shiny and plastic-y. Cemetery population: plenty. Creepy factor: moderate to light.

THE CLUES TAKE US
TO THE NECROPOLIS

To this reporter's eyes, the cemetery or the graveyard, whatever you call it, is an okay place; death is just part of life, the end part. As we were approaching, however, the weather had changed, and the moon went behind the clouds. Now the tombstones and crypts looked like the big teeth of some big dead monster. I'd just as soon go around the cemetery than go through it, but the clues took us in. Luckily, Potato didn't notice until he was well past the gates. He stopped and froze.

"Waaaaaaaiiitt a minute, Stella. This is the creamery isn't it? Stella! You got me to walk right into the creamery! I hate the creamery! No way! I'm not going in." I groaned. His constant delays were wasting valuable time. He had nothing to bargain with and hadn't figured that out yet. I shrugged and pretended not to care.

"Fine, I'll come get you when I'm done. You stay here, by the crypts full of dead people." I turned and walked off and clicked on my pen light. It took only the count of three for the expected wail.

"Stellllllaaaaaaaaaahhhhh, wait up!" He came bouncing over, whining, begging and crying as we moved through this city of the dead. One good thing about going into the cemetery is that you can use the word, necropolis, which means city of the dead, which the cemetery really is, if you think about it. Necropolis, that's an awesome word. And the dead really are here. They really are just inches away from us, the living, separated by a layer of dirt and a thin wooden box. They're all under us and around us, dressed in their Sunday best, all dried and stiff, sealed in total darkness, all just a few feet away, entombed in their coffins, hundreds of them, slowly decaying. It doesn't scare me because we'll all be there one day, the spookiest truth of all.

"Hey," Potato said, "I can't see the slime trail anymore because it's everywhere!" The little mutant was right. Slug smear was all over the place. I figured that the cemetery was either their nest, or we had just walked into a trap.

A wind had picked up and clouds of thick Tule fog flowed through the air as visibility dropped off. Fog swirled around us as we stopped. I wasn't sure which way to go because of all the confusing, crisscrossing trails. Potato wasn't pleased; and the overall creep factor received a free upgrade. We stood at the front of a small stone tomb, covered with vines and weeds. I tried to read the name of the family above the door, but it was long faded away.

All at once, Potato let out a shrill scream. I looked around. Out of the fog, three huge meat slugs slid in and surrounded us. As a reporter, was I frightened or scared by what I saw? I wouldn't say I was scared, but I was frightened, frightened of what would happen if I did get scared and this was certainly a frightening situation where one would be scared. But being scared, not that I was, makes the human body do a dramatic transformation in just seconds. Fear triggers the animal in us, so we don't think, which would waste valuable time, we just react.

A true reporter never forgets that we have evolved over billions of years, and we are really just hairless apes with cell phones and credit cards, and in some situations being an animal is helpful. So, when I need to, the cat-like Stella takes over, and I will run, and when run is blocked, then it's climb, and if climb doesn't work, then it's jump. It's pretty simple; repeat as necessary. Although lately I also have to include "drag a little tub of boy lard" with me as well, which almost doubles my weight.

There were four slugs now, the size of waterbeds, and they had quickly formed a tight ring that Potato and I were in the middle of. They moved slowly, but their mouths seemed to be able to travel over the surface of their blob bodies, so no matter where we tried to step, a slimy, open mouth was waiting. Up was the only way to go, so I leapt to the top of the gate on the small mausoleum. I wasn't sure what I was going to do about Potato when the gate I was on swung open and clobbered Potato, but he was smart enough to hang on and began to climb.

The gate swung back against the mausoleum, and we were able to jump inside, as I slammed the rusty gate shut. Inside the tiny stone room, four dusty coffins, decorated with old, dead, dried flowers were stacked neatly in the crypt. Outside, the slugs pushed at the gate, and they were surprisingly good at pushing. The old rusty bars of the gate began to bend, and slug goo came oozing through the bars as we backed against the coffins. The slugs filled the doorframe and came though the bars like fast moving Jello.

Potato bellowed, "Ahhhh, Stella! It's coming through!" Potato has a real talent for pointing out the obvious. They were indeed getting closer to us, and I was sure that they could completely squeeze though the bars, given just a few more minutes; we had to move up. We climbed on the coffins, and about half way up, Potato lost his balance and almost tumbled off the top. As he scrambled up to a stone ledge, he kicked one of the rusty metal handles on the side of the coffin. The ancient, termite-filled wood crumbled away, and the dusty coffin collapsed. The stringy corpse of a white-haired, old man crumpled to the floor like a broken chair. His skin was dried and yellow and snapped and crunched when he hit the ground. His empty eye sockets, filled with dust as his head rolled around on his thin, leathery neck. I grabbed Potato as he fought not to faint.

"Ooooooooohhhhhhh, It's not Halloween, is it?" Below us, the slugs had now squeezed into the tiny crypt, and the creatures slurped down the crunchy corpse below us. The slugs were slowly filling up the room. These creatures could obviously smell, because another slug loaf sniffed out another casket, busted through the side, and slurped down the dried corpse of a nicely dressed old woman, hat included. To this reporter's eye, it was time to go. We squeezed through a vent in the ceiling and climbed onto the roof of the small mausoleum.

9:02 p.m.: Potato was delirious as we stood on the roof of the tiny tomb, in the dead of night as the thick fog enveloped us. We were completely surrounded but were able to keep the meat slugs from coming up on the roof with a few stiff kicks. Still, it was only a matter of time before they overtook us. It was too high to jump from, and I got the feeling that these meatloaf slugs weren't alone, either. Plenty more could be out there, in the darkness.

Potato whimpered and then announced in a squeaky scream, "Well, if I'm going to be eaten, then I'm going to be full, too!" He pulled a huge wad of cold, balled up French fries from his pocket and started to shove them into his face. What a time to eat! How I loathe that little wart.

But then, below us, the meatloaf slugs began to back off and slink away. Potato was delighted. "Hey, they don't like the sound of my eating! Well, neither does my Mom, but here I go!" Potato continued to scarf down the cold fries slapping and flapping his lips even more than usual, trying to make as many eating noises as possible. It was disgusting, but the meat slugs were, in fact, retreating. I don't think his gross eating sounds made them retreat. Perhaps there was a silent signal they were tuned into; maybe they were being called back to their hive or whatever by some controlling force. Either way, after a few minutes they all quickly slithered off. We waited a bit longer and finally climbed down and, again, took off after the slug loaf thingies, this time, a lot more cautiously.

10:20 p.m.: Beyond the cemetery, the slime trail continued out and across East Booney Road. We even watched as a couple of cars briefly lost traction and skidded a little in the slug slime as the trail crossed the street and continued into the bushes.

Note: I just hate it when the trail continues into the bushes. There could be anything in those bushes, why doesn't the clue trail ever go down the sidewalk? Oh well, I continued on, determined to get the story.

FURTHER AND FURTHER
FROM HOME WE GET

We followed the trail through the night and approached a neighborhood I'd never seen before. This neighborhood wasn't like the rest of Trickle Falls; there was no glossing over this. This area was all but dead. It smelled of neglect. Only one sad streetlight flickered on the entire street. Weeds grew everywhere, lawns were bare and brown, fences were broken, dozens of wheel-less cars filled empty lots. Even an old city bus was rusting away in the middle of a weed-choked yard. Most of the houses were boarded up or gutted and abandoned. Dim lights glowed in a couple of dark windows, but, for the most part, this neighborhood was just another version of the cemetery.

We walked along following the huge slime trail. It led through an alley, around a dirt driveway and up to a huge abandoned house. The house had fancy wood trim and posts that now hung at odd angles and rotted away. I tried to make a note of the address, but the numbers and the street signs were both long gone. We crept up and surveyed the perimeter. It looked like no one had been there in years: tall weeds, boarded up windows, no signs of life, slimy or otherwise, except for their trail, which gave them away, and slipped under a battered wall at the back of the house. We couldn't squeeze under there, and even if we could, I wouldn't want to try. Who knows what was on the other side waiting for us? Whenever you are going to enter a potentially dangerous situation, you always want to keep the element of surprise and go in a way no one is expecting. Never go through the front door.

Potato was now second-guessing his desire to recover his Gamedude, so I knew I had to make a quick survey. He walked closely behind me, and when a harmless owl hooted overhead, he dug his fingernails into the back of my arms. The house was boarded up but was boarded up almost too well. There wasn't one place I could peek in. It was sealed up too tight for a house that no one cared about.

I made my way around the house, from

window to window, trying to find a sliver to look through. I spotted a low basement window; I made a note of its location. It looked like an easy entry point, if need be.

Sealed against a window, I found a sheet of plywood with a knothole in it. I took my pocketknife and popped out the knot in the wood and was able to see inside, it was apparently the kitchen. A strange yellowish glow filled the old, empty room. On the old kitchen counter, thick with dust and ruin, were about a dozen metal pans with more little meatloaves sitting in them. Apparently, Mrs. Cameron was getting ready to give all her new neighbors her special gifts. Someone had to put a stop to this.

Potato tried to peek in. He whispered, "Do you see my Gamedude?! Do you?" He tried to climb up and peek but slipped and went crashing into a pile of paint cans and yard debris. The noise shattered the night. He's such a clod. He stood up, wiping himself off. "Sorry, I—Ohhh…" The color left his face, and his eyes opened wider than I'd ever seen. I turned around, and behind us, at the top of a heap of junk, stood a giant snarling dog, baring its teeth.

Potato whispered to me in a hissing whine.

"Ooooohhhhh, Stella, it's a dog, I'm ascared of dogs!" We inched back, and this massive dog, his white fangs flashing in the night, inched down the hill, his eyes fixed on us, his growl loud and terrifying. This dog, the size of small horse, could pounce at any moment.

In slow motion, we stepped backwards millimeter-by-millimeter, time stretched, and it seemed like years. We finally rounded a short wall.

Once we hit the corner, we both just turned and ran. I worried that Potato would fall behind, but instead he passed me, running like never before. I guess he wasn't exaggerating about being afraid of dogs. After we'd cleared the street, I dared to look back and the dog was gone. I didn't know when it stopped the chase, and I didn't care. We dropped to the crumbling sidewalk and gasped for breath.

As we sat panting and gulping air, I wondered what it was that could stop these giant slugs. I needed to get in that house and see what was going on in there, but I had to be ready to protect myself and Potato. Then it hit me! I knew what we could use: a powerful chemical, sodium chloride, also known as common table salt. Everybody knows slugs hate salt; it's like the sun shining on a vampire. And what about that dog, a new, potentially dangerous player? Was the dog working with them, protecting them, being their eyes and ears since they didn't seem to have any? Then again, it didn't seem like the slugs needed eyes and ears: they had no problem almost eating Potato and a few crunchy corpses... creepy meat slug jerks.

But where on Earth could a girl like me, with a lump like Potato, get a lot of salt at near midnight? I should add another tiny detail; I was down to like five dollars, due to a whole list of reasons that are too annoying to talk about.

It took only a few seconds, but I knew it, instantly. There was only one place I could think of where I could acquire a quantity of salt, and I shuddered to think about it: the mall, the Trickle Springs Mall. Perhaps the one place in all of Trickle Falls and the rest of Bluster County that truly made my blood run cold. I had no other options, so we headed that way.

11:19 p.m.: Potato and I entered the Trickle Springs Mall at the West doors. All the stores were gated and closed up, but at the other end I could hear the piercing voices of my fellow classmates infesting the food court. The lights were blisteringly bright. Potato sniffed the air.

"Ooooooo, Stella, can I get a pretzel?"

"Yes", I replied coolly.

Potato whined and moaned. "Ooowww you never let me get anything, I-- I can? I don't think you ever let me get anything before."

"What about the French fries and the shave ice?" I asked.

"But I spent my own money."

"Yes, but I still let you." It was all part of my plan. We buy one pretzel for $1.25. That I can afford. Then we go and we add our own salt, more salt, as much as we want. There's no rule that says you can't have a lot of salt with your pretzel, and they are giving it away: it's complimentary. It's understood at every restaurant, the world over, that salt is free. There's no sign saying how much salt a paying customer can use; it's wide open.

And all the other fast food joints have free salt packets, too. We'll load up. If anyone says anything, we'll buy another pretzel or more fries. That should cover it. I explained my plan to Potato.

He, of course, was too dim to understand. "I don't like too much salt on my pretzel. If you put too much salt on, it gets tooooooo-- salty."

I could feel the anger welling up in me.

I explained that we weren't there to enjoy the pretzel-to-salt ratio. We were there to get as much salt as possible, to perhaps save our town from some sort of supernatural invasion, Trickle Falls, the most ungrateful city of all time.

"But what's the salt for?" He whined.

I explained that salt might disintegrate the meatloaf slug creatures, and we had to stop them.

"But how do you know that?"

I reminded him of when he gobbled down his fries when we were surrounded at the cemetery. It wasn't the sound of his eating, horrible as that was. It was the salt he was flinging off the fries as he wolfed them down.

He still wasn't convinced. "I don't know, these slugs are big, we'd need a lot of salt, and that would be heavy and the pretzel would be too salty. I don't think it will work. Can I get a soda too?"

INTO THE BELLY
OF THE BEAST:
THE FOOD COURT

f the mall is a giant evil monster, and it is, then the food court is the belly of that beast, and, like it or not, we were going in. Potato's whining was annoying, and I was really peeved, and I was already on my guard. So, it came as no surprise when fifth grader and brain dead punk, Bobby Bourke leaned over the fake plants and just had to say something about my investigating uniform, as I walked by.

"Ooooooweeee, well, Miss Goth, who is the funeral for?" He leaned his big fat stupid face into mine and I could smell his icky breath. I gave his right eye a nice, solid poke. "Yahhhh!" He jumped back. I answered his question.

"The funeral is for your binocular vision. Now you can take the red eye." He sat down and put some ice from his soda cup on his eye and shut up. I dress in a uniform, plain by design, which helps me blend in, and yet I wear an air of authority when questioning potential witnesses because everyone respects a uniform.

The night watchman, whose own uniform was five sizes too small for him, was standing close. The food court closed in less than forty five minutes, at midnight. This was the high point of the night watchman's shift, when he got to chase the kids out for the night. For now, around the court, kids ate food, drank sodas and talked.

My skin crawled at the little sound bites I got of their useless conversations. The standards: who likes who, and what are you wearing to the stupid dance? Ugh! The voices! "Can you believe John Mudbrain was seen kissing Jessica Spoonhead?" It's so useless. There's work to be done! The truth cannot defend itself, sadly and gladly, because I'd be out of business. Some great thinker like Charles Fort once said, "Great minds talk about new ideas; mediocre minds talk about the weather, and simple minds gossip." And it's true, and I also heard that Bobby Burke still wets the bed and even did it during a sleepover.

11:33 pm.: We made our way past Pepeto's Pasta Place, the Captain's Corny Dog stand, the Discount Dim Sum counter and Wally's Chicken Burgers, over to the pretzel stand. We were just a few meters away, almost dodging all the strange looks and ignoring the average amount of whispering and giggling. Suddenly, Judy Epstein stepped in, blocking our path.

Judy Epstein is the main reason I don't like the mall. Judy is all the tackiness of the mall in a person. She is arrogant, obnoxious, loud, brash and self-absorbed. She's also about as sincere as a grease fire. She is also the editor of *The Mallard Standard*, the award winning middle school paper and website. This reporter and Judy used to have splasher-dipper swim classes together in first grade. I pretty much saved her life during free swim once, and she's hated me ever since. I know, what was I thinking?

Judy texted on her phone the whole time we talked, RUDE. She went off like a car alarm.

"Oh my God, Stella, my guardian angel! Good to, like, totally see you. You know what? We should, like, totally hang out. What have you been doing? You look really pale. We should like, go tanning together sometime, girlfriend!"

I reminded her that many, many times I

had tried to email and had even sent her hard-copies of my stories, ready to print in *The Mallard*, and I got no response again and again.

She pretended to be concerned, but she's so fake. "Oh my God, really? You know I just got hacked and had to switch emails, so I lost a lot of stuff." Her phone rang and a lame dance club ringtone filled the food court.

"Oh my God! It's Ashley, I have to take this! But let's hang out real soon." She was off in a flash of hair, lip gloss and bling, so lame. This is the editor of *The Mallard?* She wouldn't know a good story if it had expensive shoes and bell bottoms on it. She does go downhill skiing in the winter a lot, so I can always hope.

My plan for a quick infiltration into the mall was all but ruined now. We walked up to the pretzel stand. Operating the pretzel oven was one Chuck Hansen, age 16, blonde hair, blue eyes and a wry smile with a certain something. He is a local lifeguard and pretzel vendor, obviously. He smiled and actually talked to me.

"Hey check it out; it's Stella, the Einstein of Trickle Falls. How's it going, guys?" This reporter was taken aback, that Chuck had remembered her personally. Apparently, the floor was uneven, and I lost my balance, and stumbled a bit. Luckily, my fall was saved by the ice plant and a big vase. Potato spoke up.

"We're here to get as much salt as we can, but I just want a pretzel, with the normal amount, plus mustard, and cheese dipping sauce." Chuck actually seemed amused at Potato, where all I can see is a stupid, plan-spilling, blabber mouth. Chuck spoke and his voice was surprisingly soothing to this reporter's ear.

"Salt, huh? Say, we're going to be closing soon, and I'd just throw these out anyway, so you can have these last pretzels if you want. And I'm only doing this because Stella here didn't get all agro when I babysat her and watched R rated stuff on cable." Potato did a little dance as he grabbed the last of the pretzels and stuffed them his pockets. How did Potato never learn that you don't put food in your pockets?

"Wow! Thanks, Mister!" I wasn't hungry but I had a free pretzel anyway. I wanted to be polite and needed to keep my energy up.

"What do you need salt for?" Chuck asked. I tried to craft a story in my mind, but suddenly couldn't form words. The floor in and around the pretzel stand is indeed uneven, and again, I almost slipped but recovered. I'll have to speak to the mall maintenance about that. Potato again easily spilled every detail of my plan without the slightest bit of hesitation.

"We're going to use it to kill a bunch of big slugs; I mean big slugs, which smell like meatloaf that actually started as meatloaf, which I now do not like."

"Slugs, huh? That's pretty funny, dude, nice and gross!" Chuck was amused as he cleaned the windows of the pretzel cart and took out parts to wipe down.

Potato continued, "Yeah, and we chased them from the creamery, and then we got chased by a dog. Oh, and I saw a guy with no eyeballs. I almost passed out."

I wasn't ready for such a breach of security and struggled to fix the situation and for a second considered just running for it. But before I knew it, Chuck was handing over two huge plastic bags full of salt.

"Here, take these, it's the leftover stuff from the tray. We're supposed to empty it out every night, but it's been awhile, so you're in luck. Those slugs don't have a chance."

Again, I tried to explain that I wasn't doing something as juvenile as mindlessly torturing innocent invertebrates like the common garden slug. But again, I couldn't form words and was

Chuck Hansen
*excellent former babysitter

only able to mutter a garbled, "Wow, thanks, Chuck." Chuck's cell phone rang, and gave us the perfect out. Now we had pounds of the stuff. We walked away and Chuck called out to us.

"See ya round, Stella. And keep alert, kid.

She'll teach you a thing or two. That red eye of hers sees stuff you can't imagine!" I guess a lack of water from all the running around hit me, for at that moment, my face felt flush, and I got all light headed and woozy, obviously too much salt from the pretzel and a normal reaction to some slight dehydration.

Outside the fresh air rejuvenated me as we headed for the Cavendish's. Of course Potato, that massive idiot, read the situation completely wrong and blabbed as he scarfed down his pretzel, mustard and cheese spouting from his flapping lips, and I quote:

"Stella's got a boyfriend! Stella's got a boyfriend!" I was immune to such wild accusations as Potato continued his juvenile behavior and began to croak like a stepped-on toad, "Stella and Chuck, sitting in a tree, K-I-S-S-I-N-G, first comes love, second comes marriage..." Again, I was unaffected by his childish antics, but I tripped him anyway, just to shut him up.

Regardless of what that little twerp Potato said, it would be ludicrous for this reporter to get involved with a food vendor in the course of her duty. For the record I do not love Chuck Hansen. I don't even like him! Well, I don't not like him a lot ... I mean I do like, like him, but in a nonromantical way. I hadn't even really noticed his twinkly, deep blue eyes or his perfect white teeth. And even though Chuck Hansen used to babysit me and my brothers, I am only interested in him as a potential witness or helper in my ongoing investigation.

Also, as I recall, Chuck was an excellent babysitter, so if it seems as if I admire him, it is only because I respect his skills as a babysitter and perhaps could utilize or improve on some of his techniques, babysitting techniques, I mean. I don't want to talk about it anymore, full stop.

As I suspected, upon returning to my neighborhood, the Camerons were now gone from their new house. The boxes were all strewn about in the driveway and yard, but nothing was left behind. I was sure of one thing: I hadn't seen the last of Mrs. Cameron and I could just feel it.

12:22 a.m.: We went back into Potato's house. I'd forgotten about the huge mess, but it hadn't forgot about me. Still, it would have to wait until later.

Potato made a beeline for his bedroom. "I'm beat and am going to bed!" It was going to be hard to pry him loose. But first, I needed a weapon, a delivery system to apply the salt.

I headed into Mr. Cavendish's garage for

EXHIBIT "E"

another yard implement. I knew he had what I was thinking about because I'd seen him use it, and I found it. It was the Mulch Master Yard King 2300 XL, Leaf Blower Tornado. That would be my salt delivery system. The weed whip was fine for the little meatloaf dudes, but I needed something on a science level for those big ones.

I jumped on the Cavendish's computer and looked up a map. The neighborhood from where those slugs originated was called Custard Hill, somehow fitting, but somehow not, and it wasn't that far. By my calculations we'd walked forever, and we needed to make better time. I plotted a more direct route and happily avoided another trip through the cemetery.

I ran home and got my bike as well as my detecting kit, custom-made by me. Each investigator's tool kit is as unique as she or he is. What are the key items in my detecting kit? I'm sorry, that's secret, classified information. However, one of my main tools is my custom-made detecting cards, which helps me keep track of important clues during the heat of an investigation.

I strapped the leaf blower to my bike with bungee cords and loaded the salt and some other supplies in my side baskets.

Of course, my most serious responsibility was my client, Potato. I went to his room and found him asleep in his closet, in his pajamas, zipped up in his sleeping bag, holding a tennis racquet. I spent several minutes trying to wake him, but he was totally out. I had no choice so I borrowed my Dad's baby trailer that he pulls behind his bike when he takes my little brother around. I attached the trailer to my bike and was barely able to get Potato inside the little nylon basket. Just to be safe, I duct taped Potato in place so he wouldn't fall out. He was about five times the size of my baby brother, but it would have to do. And honestly, I think Potato would have preferred to stay asleep if he had been able to choose. Finally, I was ready to face whatever it was coming from that house.

As I rode though the fog, the wind whipped at my face. The night had changed. Now it was well past midnight, and it had turned cold and mean. It was quiet except for the sound of the bike chain spinning, the pounding of this reporter's heart and Potato mumbling in his sleep.

WE ARE NOT ALONE

1 2:50 a.m.: We arrived on the deserted street, just a few blocks from the house. I took a breath and drank some water. I set out my investigating gear and took some notes and measurements and recorded them on my self-designed detecting cards.

Potato finally woke up, "Ohh! I was having the worst dream!" He looked around. "Dang. It wasn't a dream. Hey, you taped me in the trailer, awwwwwww, Stella!" I unwrapped the tape, and he flopped to the ground. "I can't wait until I'm old enough to stay at home alone! How old is that, Stella?"

I thought, as he stood up and dusted himself off. "In your case, Potato, I'd say about 19 or 20."

He dropped his head. "Dang. That's a long time from now."

I made some notes as Potato sniffed the air. Suddenly his mood instantly got better.

"Heyyyyyy! I smell barbeque." He took a huge sniff that practically rustled the trees. "I smell *really good* barbeque!" I ordered the little louse to be quiet, but it was no use. He was off like a barbeque bloodhound. I had to give chase, of course. When that guy is on to food, he can really move, that and being chased by dogs. He got away quick before I could gather up my detecting kit.

"Potato, wait!" I gave chase through a weed grown side yard between two houses. Seconds later, I heard a shriek. I was in an overgrown back yard. There was a big hedge, and I pushed through it. But my flashlight was at my bike, Blast! I must get a utility belt at some point. Flashlight or not, I still had to go after Potato.

I came through the bushes and stopped. Even though I needed to find the little spud, ASAP, I was no good without my natural night vision, so I had to stop and let my eyes adjust. Finally, I was able to see a little bit in the inky darkness. I moved around on what must have been the back yard and patio area of this house. The house looked like it might have been nice in another time, but now it looked like an experiment in neglect. The big yard was littered with junk and makeshift greenhouses, sheds, tall weeds and old dead appliances. Attached to the house was a large covered patio. Huge overgrown plants wrapped around it, but noises were definitely coming from within, so I moved in.

I moved through a maze of old boxes, rusty yard furniture and stacks of stuff. In the darkness I heard noises: gross, wet, squishing noises, and yet the air smelled sweet and tangy. In the darkness, I turned, and from deep in the shadows, a pair of red eyes glared at me, fixed on me. Smoke filled the patio area and was coming from around the figure of a thin, old man. He hovered over a glowing flame watching me, the fire light flickering in his eyes. He was obviously mad, and his long thin face twitched with anger. In the dim light, he pulled up something in his hand, something shiny and metal, that reflected the fire in front of him. Was it a weapon? I stepped back, closed my eyes and fired a shot from my camera. He was momentarily blinded.

"Argh! Now I can't see a thing! What is this?" He groaned, "Grand Central Terminal? I can't feed the whole freakin' block. Well, I can. In fact, no one can feed the block like me. Have a seat. Help yourself. What do you like? Chicken or steak? Oh and I've also got some corn on the cob."

My eyes adjusted to the dim room. The whole area was once a beautiful patio. Now overgrown, in its day it would have been a great place to entertain loads of guests if you like that sort of thing. Now, however, it was a shambles, littered with broken lawn furniture, a weed filled fountain, torn and tattered umbrellas, moldy cushions and overgrown planters. The old man worked behind the barbeque that chugged out smoke as he flipped some meat. The squishing gross noises were of course, again, Potato eating as he sat at a little table with a tattered checkered tablecloth.

"Stella! You should try this! This barbeque chicken is great!" Forget about being poisoned; he would just dive in and eat anything put in front of him. I demanded an explanation from this mystery man who demanded an explanation from us being on his property.

Potato volunteered an answer. "We're going to go find those giant meatloaf slugs and get my Gamedude back. We followed their gooey trail, and it brought us over here, to their nest."

"Bad idea." The man said and stepped out from behind the barbeque. He was missing his right arm at the elbow. His sleeve was neatly tied up below where his arm should be. He was also missing his left leg above the knee. He hopped from place to place, and set some more food on the table as he spoke.

"Marvin T. Atwater is the name. I've lived here forty-six years, but it's all for shot now. Trust me, you don't want any part of those slug creatures. They're dangerous."

"I know!" Potato interrupted, "It tried to eated me, but Stella drove it off, but my Gamedude was in my back pocket and fell out inside the slug!"

Mr. Atwater hobbled around and ferried out more delicious food for us. "Gamedude, huh? What game were you playing?" He asked Potato.

"*The Indigo Princess: Xula 3, Destiny's Ring.*" Marvin thought about it and asked,

"Did you already capture the leprechauns?"

"Yes…" Potato was getting worried. I wondered why this two-limbed old man knew so much about *Indigo Princess*.

"Have you made it to the inner circle of harmony with the gilded scoop?" Marvin asked.

"Almost, I just needed a few more diamond eggs." Marvin seemed to know all about Gamedudes and video games. The conversation was getting annoying.

"Did you save your game before it was swallowed by the giant slug?" Potato got more agitated. He stopped eating for a second and whimpered,

"I don't remember."

Marvin shook his head. "That's too bad, boy, that's a really hard level to have to do over…"

I butted in, "Look, what are you doing, barbequing for no one?"

Marvin hobbled back behind the barbeque and flipped some more chicken on the grill. "Well, I'm leaving; I can't stay in this neighborhood one night longer." The fire flamed up around his grill. The old man was thoughtful. I took good notes.

"I used to be the barbeque king out here, every weekend, and almost every night in summer! This whole street would just fill with friends and neighbors, and everyone would bring a dish, and we'd play games and talk, listen to music, dance and have great barbeque. I won top prize three years running at the State Fair for my sauce and five years running for my chicken wings alone, a record that still hasn't been broken. Ten years ago, a local TV show came and did a segment from there, right where you're standing. But now it's all gone, all ruined. So I'm out of here, and I'm the last one. Curse those things, but it's not all their fault; they're just the nail in the coffin for this neighborhood."

He hopped over and fastened a homemade wooden leg onto his stump. "I had some meat in the freezer, thought I'd 'que it up like the old days, then load up the ol' car and hit the road. A lot of people will barter for good barbeque."

To this reporter, Mr. Atwater was a suspicious character. He hobbled around, with his peg leg and his stump arm, but for some reason, I still didn't feel sorry for him. He suddenly got angry: "This is what those slugs did to me! That's it! I'm leaving before there's nothing left to leave, not one more night in this place."

Potato was taken by this story. "Wow, that's terrible mister," now filling his face with ribs, "I got inside one of those slugs too, but it just sort of swished me around like a breath mint, I guess."

Marvin turned over his steaks and a fire roared around him. "You got lucky, kid!" I was suspicious of Marvin's story. Why would anyone hang around after getting a limb eaten off? And how could a grown man lose two limbs to a slug that couldn't even begin to digest Potato in the four minutes or so that he was inside one?

Marvin continued to rant. "Lousy slug monsters got me while I was sleeping! I woke up one night and bam! I'd lost a limb. The second time, I awoke and looked down and thought, 'Not again!'"

His story was about as put together as a soup sandwich, but I was a guest, after all, and the chicken was really good. So, I politely asked, "Mr. Atwater, why didn't you call the police when you got attacked?"

He slunk away. "Nahhhh, I got a record for some non-barbeque related mistake I made years and years ago. I can't go to the cops, so-- I guess I'll just go."

I continued to try and figure out his story. "Did you tell the hospital what happened when you got attacked?"

He laughed and took a big swig of barbecue sauce. "I didn't go to no doctor. I just did it the old barbeque way -- just dunked it in sauce and then stuck it in the fire, and it stumped up real nice-like. Hurt like the dickens, though." He wagged his arm stump at us.

Potato stopped eating mid-bite. He pushed the plate away and wiped his mouth on his shirt.

He looked a little queasy. "You stuck your

stumps in that fire, in that barbeque, right there?" Marvin gave him a wink. "The same barbeque that you just cooked all this meat on, that I just ate?!" Marvin gave Potato another wink. Potato swallowed hard and turned a little green.

I continued to interrogate the witness. "What do you think these meatloaf slugs are?" I asked.

"I have no idea. All I know is that you shouldn't go in there; it's a bad place." I quizzed him about Mrs. Cameron, when the slugs first appeared, times and dates, but numbers just confused him. He never saw any woman poking around that house; he only saw a little man that might have actually been a monkey. The witness also stated that he first saw the slugs or signs of the slugs either a few weeks ago or three years ago or 22 years ago. He was an unreliable witness.

"Well, it's about twenty-seven thirty," he said. "And I got the car all loaded, and I want to hit the road tonight, and if you're smart, you'll do the same." We thanked him for the food and left Mr. Atwater's patio as he poured water on his barbeque and wrapped up the last of his cooking in tin foil.

Outside of the patio, we stuck to the far ends of the backyards as we moved along, from yard to yard. I carried the leaf blower in front of me. I had stuffed the wind barrel with salt and put a sock over the front of it with holes in it, so that the salt would be slowly sprayed out. Potato carried the rest of the salt on his shoulder in the two bags tied together.

SEARCH AND DESTROY

We stuck to the backsides of the yards as we worked our way over. We got within a few meters of the house when we heard the one sound we really didn't want to hear: that growl, the unmistakable growl of an angry dog. That dog must be some sort of telepathic guard for the slug monsters. We tried to be quiet, but he'd already spotted us from across an empty lot. Fortunately, the dog was at least a hundred meters away. We made a run for it and followed the slime trail back to the house. We ran to the small basement window I'd seen before. I pushed the old window, and it came out of the frame and dropped inside. I tossed in the leaf blower and started to slide into the tiny window.

The dog was much quicker than I'd anticipated, and it closed the hundred meters in a split second. The pounding of his huge paws in the dirt grew louder and louder as it approached. Potato moved faster than I've ever seen him and didn't bother to wait for me to get through the window, and instead, tried to dive in at the same time, head-first. It was too narrow of a space, and in an instant, we were both stuck, my head and arm sticking out and his legs sticking out next to me.

The massive dog approached at full speed, his growl turning to a roar, and for all my might, I just couldn't move. I covered up as I expected to get my face bitten off, but it never came. Slowly I uncovered and looked. The dog had stopped at the edge of the yard and wouldn't come any further. It snarled and growled at us and hopped around but wouldn't come near the house. As I watched, his snarl turned into a whine and finally a whimper. What a strange thing for a dog to do.

I relaxed, and Potato relaxed, and we both dropped into the room. I popped on my flashlight. We were in a small workroom full of old house debris: pieces of wood, rolls of wall-paper, piles of junk. Potato crouched down. He was shaking. I may have broken him this time, between the slugs and the dog. He sat in the corner, wide eyed and worried. I decided that perhaps Potato needed a break from the action.

We sat quietly to see if anything stirred with our not-so-silent arrival. We listened: nothing. This dim room seemed safe, so I decided that he would stay there. I would scout ahead and come back for ammo as needed. I gave him a glow stick, cracked it, and lit up the room. He seemed fine with that and found a box to hide under. I was bending my main rule, but it was either that or bend his brain.

I would come back in five minutes and adjust our plan from there. I didn't want to use the door, so I pushed out behind an old rotten wall. Inside the hall more dust and debris, peeling wallpaper, and broken boards lay strewn about. Slime trails went everywhere. Like, I didn't already know, but this was definitely the nest: the air was thick and steamy and smelled bad.

First, I tied my flashlight to the leaf blower. Then, I opened the top on a small bottle of glow-in-the-dark paint from my kit. It's a simple trick, dripping tiny drops of glow in the dark paint, so I can find my way out, even in total blackness if that were to happen. I taped the bottle to my ankle and moved in.

I would like to point out that although salt does kill slugs and snails, it's a brutal way to be killed. I only use salt on giant, evil slugs who masquerade as meatloaves. Regular slugs are a normal part of nature and deserve to be respected and, if not respected, then at least just left alone. Slugs have a right to slide along just like anyone else. However, if they grow to the size of a tent full of Jello and eat fish, Gamedudes, cats, and goofy little whiny kids, then yes, it's OK to dispatch them with salt.

THROUGH THE EYE
OF THE NEEDLE

After setting up my camera, I crept along in the darkened hallway, keeping a sharp eye and moving silently. The basement was a dark labyrinth of little rooms, closets, hallways and stairwells. I rounded a corner and stopped. The room up ahead glowed with the same sickly yellow glow I'd seen though the kitchen window. Worse yet, the giant slug loaves were everywhere. There must have been ten of them just in the hall, piled in doorways and against the walls.

I started to shake uncontrollably. It was too much for me. I hadn't tried my weapon, and I didn't really have a back up if it didn't work. I thought of Charles Fort, and it was a little comforting and then for some reason, I thought of Chuck. I wanted out. This was too much for my brain; I was aborting the mission.

I started to step back, but it was too late. One of them had noticed me and moved quicker than before. It was now or never. I pulled the ripcord and the leaf blower did nothing. I pulled again. Did it have gas? I gave it a shake and pulled again. It wouldn't start. I now had the attention of all the slugs in the hall, and they all quickly moved toward me, a huge wall of goo coming down the hall. The boards cracked, and the walls creaked and peeled as the mass of slugs came at me. I stepped back and pulled again, nothing. I looked at the leaf blower and found a choke button; I gave it a squeeze and pulled again.

The leaf blower sputtered to life. I pulled the trigger, and the salt flew in a fast, deadly spray. The salt crystals hit the slugs, and instantly liquified their skin and kept going.

They shrieked and roared as I sprayed the salt. Halves of slugs tried to slither away, but I was on them. Finally, destruction had come for these evil whatevers. Slug goo began to flow! It worked perfectly, and I had them on the run, when I abruptly ran out of salt.

I ran back to the tiny room we had come in through and opened the door. Potato was gone; and a slime trail told the whole story. Dang, they had got him. I rooted around where he had been, and discovered that he had been smart enough to hide the bags of salt. I grabbed my camera, loaded up the leaf blower, threw the bags over my shoulder and charged back down into the depths of this horrible nightmare to recover my client.

POTATO IN TROUBLE AGAIN !!

I crept through the room I had just liquefied. I moved down a dark hallway. I listened. The slugs didn't seem to have any sort of telepathic capabilities because I didn't hear any sounds of alarm or alert up ahead. I tip-toed down the stairs and walked into a low ceilinged cellar that was steaming hot and stuffed with slug creatures, hundreds of them. My creep factor was off the scale, and my legs wanted to run as fast as I could, but I knew I had only minutes to save Potato. The room was quiet and still. None of them seemed active. I switched off my flashlight and crept up; the slug monsters seemed to be in some sort of sleep state.

Time was running out. Potato was probably inside one of those things. How on earth was I going to find him, and what if I salted one with him in it? Would he be melted too? This was a bad situation. I gingerly tip-toed through the field of slugs that slowly oozed and wiggled in their fitful sleep.

There were so many slugs and so many rooms. It seemed hopeless. There was no way I could find him in time. He just couldn't hang on that long. I moved through the next room and down a hall. I wanted to run, but I had to go slow and quiet. Sure the salt worked fine, but there was no way that I had enough to liquefy all these beasts, not even close. I'd have needed five pretzel stands worth; that's how many there were.

I stepped into another room with a few of the dormant slugs. They all looked the same! I almost ran out to look elsewhere when I smelled something different but familiar, something from earlier when things weren't so crazy. I sniffed the air. It was the smell of asparagus! I looked around on the floor, and a sure enough, one of the slugs had a little puddle. Potato had peed!

Wasting no time, I coated my hand in salt and punched it into the head of the slug. It shrieked and opened its mouth. I grabbed Potato's ankles and for the second time in one night, yanked him out of a giant slug. He slid out and slapped against the wall. He was slick with goo, and old newspapers and dirt stuck to the slime all over him.

He sat up and held up his hand. "Look, I found my Gamedude." He wiped his eyes and face of goo. The rest of the slugs were now awake and cranky. I fired up the leaf blower and cut loose. Within a minute, the room was just goo, 15 centimeters deep.

"Wow!" Potato yelled, "That really works!" I got Potato to his feet. We rounded the corner, and the hall was completely blocked by the slugs; easily five meters deep. I didn't know if the leaf blower had that kind of fire power. I got ready to pull the trigger, when without warning, the whole world erupted downward.

For a second I didn't know what had happened. I could hear falling boards and taste thick dust. I felt for the leaf blower and switched on my light. The dust was settling and I looked up. The floor had collapsed under the weight of all those slugs. Now I was in some sort of sub-basement. I heard Potato cough. I hopped up and fished him out of the heap. There were still huge slugs moving under all'the debris, and we leapt up and ran off the pile of broken floor. We crawled through a big hole in the wall into another huge room. It glowed with that strange yellow glow and steam filled the air. Potato was glued to my back.

In the center of the room, the dirt floor was broken away, large boulders and jagged rocks pushed up through the twisted concrete floor. Steam and gases wafted out of this unusual geological event. I'd found the source of the yellow light, all right. It was some form of energy coming from this fissure, cutting deep into the earth. How deep? I never got close enough to see. I would estimate this crevice was five to nine meters long and two meters wide at its widest. It looked like a giant wound in the floor, and dozens and dozens of small hamster sized meat slugs were slowly inching up and out.

Potato had his eyes sealed shut. "Owwww, Stella, I hate it here."

From behind us, something made a squishing sound. I looked back; we were surrounded. Potato sealed his eyes shut even tighter. "Now I hate it even more." I decided to do the humane thing first, and I wanted to see if these things had any intelligence or if they were just mindless drones, directed by someone else, namely Mrs. Cameron, whoever or whatever she was.

"See this!" I yelled, holding up the puttering leaf blower. For a moment, all the slugs did pause at the sound of my voice. "This is full of salt. Now, if you-- things let us out, I won't have to destroy any more of you." I waited for some sign of recognition. Nothing, no sign of anything. Then all together, they all started to slither toward us again. I had no choice. I cut loose and the salt flew. The slugs popped and disintegrated like big water balloons filled with gunk. They turned and twisted and tried to get away, but the salt made them turn from a thing to a puddle in just a second or two, with plenty of bubbling and foamy grossness. Goo sprayed and splattered everywhere. I burned through the first bag of salt and reloaded several times with the other.

We charged around, spraying as many as we could as the entire place went crazy. We ran upstairs and sprayed there too.

The sound of the slugs roaring and shrieking was deafening. A few slugs were trying to climb a large support beam in the middle of the room, and I blasted them good. The goo from the creatures splashed on the electrical fuse box, which crackled and zapped. Sparks flew into the room as black smoke puffed out, and the fuse box quickly burst into flames. The splashed slug goo easily caught fire, too. So, these things were flammable. Now we really had to get out immediately. If all that goo caught fire, we'd be roasted alive, with extra salt.

I shook the leaf blower, and it felt like I had one good burst of salt left, and that was it. There was a flight of stairs at the far end of the room. Between us were at least 10 meters of angry slugs coming our way. Instead of trying to wipe them all out, I cut a path on the floor through the slug creatures. Potato and I ran for it and slid across the slick floor and leapt onto the stairs. We clanged up into an old pantry room and raced through the house, which was quickly filling with smoke and burning embers. I saw a hint of the streetlight through where the screen door would have been. Potato and I flung ourselves against the old boarded up plywood. Luckily, it gave way, and we toppled out.

We busted out of the house and were in the yard. We had made it out. After breathing dust, burning house smoke, slug steam and salt, I was ripping thirsty and dashed toward the pool, ready to even drink pool water. Naturally, the empty old pool was all busted and cracked, and the deep end was filled with weeds and awful pool scum. Great, just great.

Smoke now chugged from the roof of the house on Custard Hill. The shrieks of the dying slugs were eerie, and I almost felt sorry for them, but not quite.

Puffing and panting, Potato rolled over, slick with sludge. Strangely he looked comfortable at the edge of an old empty pool. He pulled his gooey Gamedude up to his face and wiped off the screen. "Owwwwwwwwwww, I didn't save my game. Now I have to start the level over. Dang it."

I gulped for fresh air and tried to calm down when something caught my attention out of the corner of my eye. The pond of stagnant water in the deep end of the broken swimming pool began to churn and splash, and in an instant, a giant slimy slug rose out of the mucky water. This slug was ten times bigger than the ones that attacked us in the house, and the ground trembled and shook. I scrambled to my feet, but Potato was already in trouble; he had fallen forward into the empty pool and was gripping the sides.

"Stella! Help!!!" His fingers popped off the edge, and he began to slide into the deep end of the empty pool, heading toward the slimy water that splashed and foamed around the base of this giant slug. I jumped in and slid down next to him. The entire pool was slick with goo, and we couldn't keep in place. No matter how we tried, we just kept sliding closer toward the massive, writhing slug. It could sense us, or smell us, because its huge mouth roared and drooled at our feet. Potato screamed and howled, and this reporter indeed wondered if she'd ever be able to file this final report. Then a loud, steady voice called out in the night.

"I'll take care of this one!"

To my surprise and great relief, Marvin Atwater was standing on the diving board behind this whale sized slug.

"Hey, remember me?" Marvin hollered and leapt off the diving board and plunged his crutch and peg leg into the back of the giant slug's head. The giant slug monster surged ten meters in the air, roared with anger and tried to fling Marvin off.

Marvin screamed at the creature as he hung on. "You don't like salt, huh? Well then you'll hate my Custard Hill Special Barbeque Salt! Try this on, sluggy!" He stabbed at the back of the slug's head with his crutch and poured his barbeque salt into the gooey wound. On contact, the salt bubbled and frothed. The ground shook as this massive monster thrashed around. The pool cracked, the water in the deep end splashed and sprayed, and the roar was like nothing I've ever heard.

The meat slug was completely freaking out. It moved faster than I ever thought possible for a giant thing. Still, Potato and I struggled to get a grip on the goo-slicked pool. Thousands of pounds of meatloaf slime were writhing in the air above us. If it slammed down, we'd be instantly crushed.

Suddenly a loud clang caught my attention. I looked back toward the shallow end, and the dog had returned and had nosed a rusty lounge chair to the edge of the pool. The headrest on the chair was caught on the metal ladder, and I was able to reach out and just barely get a grip on the chair frame. I grabbed Potato's arm with my free hand, and we slowly worked our way to the edge of the pool and were finally able to climb out.

Atwater yelled as he rode the back of the Slug, "Mess with me, huh? Eat my favorite arm and leg, will you? You didn't actually think I was just going to sit back and do nothing, did you? You are more stupid than you look, Mr. Meat Slug!"

The creature writhed and thrashed out of the pool and crashed through a fence and a shed and then down into the gulley behind the neighborhood. I heard Mr. Atwater yelling at it all the way down. "You messed with the wrong Barbeque-ist! I was block champion, five years running, five year running!" The strange noises continued and finally faded away as they disappeared into the night.

M.T. ATWATER VS. SLUG!

In the firelight from the burning house, Potato and I climbed out of the slippery pool and lay on the ground in front of the dog. We all just sat there, all of us panting and looking at each other. I immediately realized I'd read the dog all wrong. From the first time we came through here, he wasn't trying to hurt us: he was trying to warn us, protect us, keep us away.

I carefully petted him, and he seemed to like it. His large tail even wagged just a little. Potato petted him as well.

"Say, this is neat. I never been around a dog that wasn't trying to bite me before. He's pretty cool. I think maybe I want to be a dog when I grow up." In every way, it's perfect that I call him Potato.

The house was really on fire now; flames roared from the roof, and in the distance I could hear the sound of fire trucks approaching. The dog was gone once we got up and around. I didn't see him go. But I know I'll see him again, around the neighborhood, around town. I named him Stranger. Thanks for the hand, Stranger.

We loaded up the leaf blower onto my bike, and Potato and I guzzled water from the water bottles in my bike baskets. We headed down through the gully in the opposite direction that

Mr. Atwater had gone. Above us, on the road, fire trucks raced back to Custard Hill.

Potato was delirious as we rode, but he was alive and happily babbled on. "Wow, I was eaten twice by a big meatloaf. First time, it was feet first, then head first, and I prefer feet first. No, actually I prefer not at all. And then we were chased by a dog, but we got free pretzels, and then we got free barbeque, and then I got eaten but found my Gamedude but then fell through a floor, but my game wasn't saved!"

We rode back to our own neighborhood and the cool fresh air felt good on our faces. We arrived back at the Cavendish's house and destroyed kitchen.

2:55a.m.: I finished the last of the cleaning; it's cleaner than when I got there. It was a big job, and I was surprised how much Potato helped too until he fell asleep standing up. I finally put him to bed.

I took more than enough slug samples for further analysis. I was also able to get rid of the rest of the slug parts in all the Cameron's moving boxes that filled the dumpster. A drinking glass and a plate or two were broken, but they'll

never notice. Just moments after I finished, Mrs. Cavendish came home, all smiles and laughing. She paid me well and I wandered home.

All this and I still had my regular homework. I used to have to brief little maniacs like Potato on keeping their mouths shut when the inexplicable happened. Heck, I'd even bribe the little snots with ice cream or video games or staying up late, but actually, I was over-reacting all along.

Not that long ago, I realized this problem wasn't a problem at all. Go ahead, tell your parents exactly what we did; tell anybody! Tell everybody! They don't believe me when I provide photographic proof, they are certainly not going to believe you, not in a million years.

EPILOGUE

This was a truly complex case, and it feels far from over. It is this reporter's opinion that perhaps the collapsing house blocked the fissure from which the creature came, or did it? If all those critters were as flammable as the first, then they all could have all been easily cooked in that blaze. But were any outside of the nest? It seems to me that even one of those, out there, could cause real trouble. And what does it take to block a fissure in the earth, anyway? I will have to monitor it, very closely.

And what of Mr. Marvin T. Atwater? What to make of the dog, Stranger, a new canine ally perhaps? And who knew that yard equipment would play such an important role in the controlling of the supernatural? It all goes in the report and on the blog.

So many unanswered questions: what was

the connection between Mrs. Cameron and the meat loaf monsters? And what is the connection between Mrs. Cameron and the Cavendish's? Why here, why just two doors down from me? There are a lot of details I need to record on my blog. I also need to rethink important facts and clues while they're fresh in my mind. With every question answered, ten more questions were asked. Come to think of it, I didn't really answer any, just yet.

I also downloaded the pictures from the night and studied the one of Mrs. Cameron and her cat, but on close inspection, I was shocked to see that it wasn't a cat that Mrs. Cameron was stroking. It was a slug. In the picture she's treating a slug like a baby. I hate babies, and I hate killer slugs.

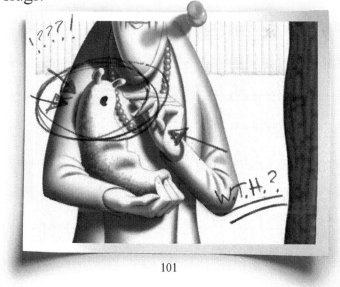

It is, however, interesting to note that I, a seasoned investigator, who takes the unusual and the strange head-on, would see what I thought was a cat.

So strange was that image of this old woman holding a baby meat slug that my brain wouldn't see it, wouldn't recognize the impossible. Just more proof on how vigilant I must be in seeking the truth. Sometimes things are so strange, I can't even trust my own eyes. Note to myself: always take lots of pictures.

All in all, it turned out to be a truly unexpected sequence of events in the ever changing process of good investigating. As they used to say in the olden detective days, "A mystery is a foot chopped off and not claimed by the owner."

So, if you're out there, dear reader, kicking around in the back waters of the Internet, looking for a truth that might leave you uneasy and unable to sleep, look no further than my investigations. If you're brave enough to open your eyes and forget what you think you know about reality, you might have come to the right place. Do you really want to know what's really going on? Some people don't, but this reporter does, and that's why I do the work I do. And beyond just knowing is also being ready, ready for whatever might leap out of the shadows and come for you. Information is power, so stay informed on the strange goings-on as they continue to go on.

I wanted to get "The red eye express.com," but it was taken, so instead, check out the whole truth at www.stellasbabysittingservice.com.

This case is to remain open until further notice. This report faithfully submitted by Stella Louise Sedgwick, investigator and, ugh, babysitter.

Stella's Detecting Cards

Case #	Date	Time

☐ Day
☐ Night
Weather   Visibility

Event or Activity

Description
_____
_____
_____
_____
_____

☐ Man made ☐ Natural ☐ Supernatural ☐ Unknown

Witness(es)   phone/email
_____
_____
_____

Suspects/Suspicions
_____
_____
_____
_____

Evidence
_____
_____
_____
_____
Collected? YES/NO

Refer case to:
T.B.D. ☐
Parents ☐
Pincipal ☐
Police ☐
Newspaper ☐
Pentagon ☐

Attach additional pages as needed.

Case #	Date	Time

Primary Witness(es)

Witness Evaluation

_____
_____
_____
_____
_____

☐ Credible ☐ Incredible ☐ Impossible ☐ Baloney

Witness Statement

_____
_____
_____
_____
_____

Scene Map

_____
_____
_____

Conclusions

_____
_____
_____
_____

Solved? YES/NO

Attach additional pages as needed.

27146569R00060

Made in the USA
San Bernardino, CA
26 February 2019